# Finding Beauty in Disaster

*A Novel*

## Written By
## Allison Searson

**Finding Beauty in Disaster**
**ISBN:** 978-1-7346285-5-5

Printed in the United States of America

## Acknowledgements

I would like to thank God, my Father the Giver of the gift for blessing me with this beautiful story and opportunity. I would also like to thank my parents, sister, and entire family for always believing in me, supporting me, and seeing all that God has placed in me. A special thanks to my grandfather, Elder James Lucas Sr., who has now gone on to be with Jesus, for always speaking into my life the things that God showed him about me. And last, but certainly not least, I would like to thank my amazing publisher Robin Major-Oliphant of One2Mpower publishing for pushing me and helping to bring my vision to life. A special thanks to all of my supporters for supporting me, purchasing my materials, and for doing life with me. I LOVE you all! To God be ALL the glory!

-Allison

"To all who mourn in Israel, he will give a crown of beauty for ashes, a joyous blessing instead of mourning, festive praise instead of despair. In their righteousness, they will be like great oaks that the Lord has planted for his own glory."
Isaiah 61:3 (NLT)

*He's trading beauty for your ashes.*

## Intro

Have you ever felt like you had it all? I mean, like you had everything you could ever imagine: fine husband, a beautiful home, beautiful children, and lived a lavishly wealthy lifestyle. You're on cloud nine, and then in a single moment, within a blink of an eye, you lose it all. Everything you worked so hard to maintain, gone in an instant. That once happy lifestyle just disappears—no warning, no heads up. Messed up, isn't it? Well, welcome to my world. My name is NaTasha, and this is the story of my life. I'm going to share with you how God traded beauty for my ashes.

# Prologue

Aaron and I had always been together. We grew up together, went to school together, and were high school sweethearts. We got married during my second year of college. I was twenty, and he was twenty-two. Everyone thought we were too young to get married, but we didn't care because we were in love.

I remember my mother being livid when I told her I was dropping out of college to move away to New York City to be with Aaron. She couldn't understand why I was putting my dreams on hold to follow him. She said I was making the biggest mistake of my life, but at the time, I thought she was talking nonsense. The whole reason we were going to New York City was so he could produce a play he wrote. I mean, how could marrying the man of my dreams at the age of twenty, and moving to New York City be the biggest mistake of my life? We were wealthy and happy, so that was all that should have mattered, right? Fast forward ten years and two kids later, and I would soon see my mother was right.

Travel back in time with me, twenty years to be exact, and you will see how God allowed me to find beauty in disaster.

# Chapter 1
## *Everything Falls Apart*

It was January 1, 1999, the year that marked ten years Aaron and I had been married. I asked him if he wanted me to make his favorite meal like I did every year, but he said it wouldn't be necessary. I thought he was planning something special to mark the occasion, so I didn't mention it again. I figured he wanted it to be a surprise since I had a special surprise for him as well. So, I headed out to pick up our sons Corbin, 7, and Calvin, 2, from his mother's house.

"Hey, Mommy!" said Corbin and Calvin.
"Hey, boys! I am so happy to see you. How was your time with grandma?"
"It was great! We made chocolate chip cookies," Corbin said.
"I see because it's all over your face."
"Mama Campbell, thank you for keeping the boys."
"Uh-huh," she said.
Something seemed odd with her, but I didn't want to pry, so I just ignored it.
"Mommy, where's Daddy?" asked Corbin.
"He's at home waiting for us, sweetheart."

"Okay, Mommy. I can't wait to see him!"

We had no idea we were in for a rude awakening once we got home. I pulled into our neighborhood. Calvin was asleep, and Corbin was going on and on about how he wanted to tell his dad what he did at Nana's house. I was listening to Corbin talk but got distracted when I saw a huge U-Haul truck in our driveway. "What? Aaron didn't tell me we were moving. Maybe he bought us a new house for our anniversary?" Nevertheless, I unloaded the boys from the car and walked into the house. "Aaron?" I hear nothing. I walk into the living room and see a strange woman and a little boy sitting on my couch.

The little boy appeared to be the same age as Corbin. He glanced and started pointing at us as he whispered something to the woman. Corbin approached the boy, and the two started playing as if they were best friends. Calvin was still asleep in my arms. The woman looked up from a magazine she was reading, and we made eye contact. Confused, I plastered on a smile and said, "Hello, you must be one of Aaron's clients. I'm NaTasha, his wife." When she heard me say I was Aaron's wife, she rolled her eyes and looked disgustedly at me. I heard

Aaron come into the living room on the phone with someone. As soon as the woman heard his voice, she stood up with her hand on her hip. I could see she was pregnant and appeared to be wearing one of my rings!

"Aaron, what is going on?! You called me over here to have me waiting in the living room for over an hour? Don't you know we have somewhere to be within the next thirty minutes?!" the woman yelled.

"Felicia, just relax. I've had some important business I needed to take care of."

I stood in the living room, confused. They were acting as if my children and I weren't even in the room. Who is Felicia? And, how do she and Aaron know each other?

"Aaron, honey, why is there a U-Haul truck in the middle of our driveway? Also, who is this woman? Is she one of your clients?"

Felicia mocked me and said, "One of his clients? Please! Honey, I'm his fiancé. You and your rug rats are moving out, and I'm moving in! Chile, he is giving you the boot. You two are over, Aaron and I are in love, and we're going to be welcoming our second child into this world."

My eyes filled with tears at the sound of this. I looked at Aaron in disbelief. He wouldn't even look at me and stared at the floor the entire time Felicia was talking. Finally, he looked me in the eyes and said, "It's true. All of it is true. I'm filing for a divorce. Felicia and I have been seeing each other for the past seven years. We have a son together, and we're expecting our second child. I'm sorry you had to find out this way, I've been meaning to tell you for a while. I'm just not in love with you anymore. The majority of your stuff has been packed up and loaded in the U-Haul truck. You have thirty minutes to get the rest of your things and get out."

Tears started streaming down my face. Corbin looked at his father with a hurt and confused expression on his face.

"What?! Aaron, I love you! How could you do this to me? I am your wife! Seven years...you've been cheating on me for seven years?! That's more than half of our marriage. How could you do this to me? On New Year's Day...it's our anniversary! Why would you lead me to believe you were in love with me all this time? What about our sons? How do you think they will feel once they are old enough to understand what took place? What about them?"

"I'm sure you will manage," Aaron said.

"Aaron! I can't believe you. I am pregnant. How could you do this to me, your sons, and your unborn daughter?"

Aaron appeared to have formed tears in his eyes at the sound of "daughter," yet he quickly dismissed whatever feelings he had.

"Again, I am sure you will manage. All of Corbin and Calvin's things have been packed and loaded as well. To show you I'm not completely heartless, here are keys and information to an apartment where you will now be staying. I've paid the first six months' rent, so that should help you until you get on your feet since you don't work. You may also keep your car since you may need it to live in after your rent expires. With no degree, it's pretty tough to find a decent job out here, especially since you'll now be responsible for three kids," Aaron glanced at his watch. "Don't bother coming back over here. I'm changing the locks as soon as you leave. Here's a thousand dollars to get you started. Don't bother using the debit or credit cards we once shared because I froze those accounts. Now, you really need to hurry and gather the rest of your things. Felicia and I have important things to do, and we must be on our way."

I literally picked myself up off the floor. Corbin was crying for his dad. Calvin, now awake, was screaming at the top of his lungs. I tried to gather my thoughts. I felt a mixture of emotions: stupid, humiliated, abandoned, and unloved. I had no family in New York, and all my family members were in California. I had no college degree, no work experience. I had always been a stay-at-home mom, a housewife, how was I going to provide for myself and three kids?

I gathered the rest of my things I could carry. At this point, the U-Haul driver was agitated. I gave him the address to the apartment, and he angrily pulled off while I loaded my sobbing boys into my car. This was their home. We were a family. This was all they knew. I pulled off sadly from the driveway and could see Felicia laughing and waving in my rearview mirror. Tears streamed down my face. How could this have happened to me? I always thought I was the luckiest woman in the world like God had smiled on me. Why would God do this to me? Why would he put my children and I through such horrible pain?! God, why have You forsaken me? Why did You give me this man and lavish lifestyle, just to take it all away? I can't do this! I can't do this! Not on my own, I can't! God, I need you! I need you more now than ever!

# Chapter 2
## *Where Do We Go from Here?*

It's been four months since I was served my divorce papers. I don't even know how Aaron managed to get them served so quickly. I am also four months pregnant with a baby girl but have an appointment with my gynecologist tomorrow morning for an abortion. I hated myself for even thinking of having an abortion, but I couldn't bear the pain of carrying and delivering that man's child after what he did to me. I'm at my worst, and I don't see how I could come up from here. I hated that Corbin and Calvin had to see me this way. I'm depressed and completely stressed out! I can't think straight, and I don't know how much more I can take! It has gotten to the point where I even believed the world would be much better off without me, and I thought I should just end it all, but I couldn't. I have two boys who need me. They need their mother, but I wasn't feeling like her. I wasn't myself. I had no one to turn to. Aaron's family had completely shut me out. I don't know what he told them, but now, it doesn't even matter.

I had a hard time finding a job. No one would hire me. They didn't want to take a chance on someone in the big city with no work experience, plus being pregnant didn't help. Money was running low, and the fridge was empty. It was either eat or fill up the tank with gas. I believe in God, but I don't feel like He was hearing me. Does He see me? Does He know what I'm going through? Does He even care? Deep down, I know He does, but my circumstances tell me otherwise. I feel like I should call my mom, but I don't want to. I don't want to hear, "I told you so!" I just don't want her to know. I want her to believe I was okay. I want her to believe everything was fine, but it wasn't. I couldn't go on like this. I had to give her a call. Here goes nothin'. The phone keeps ringing and ringing, and my heart is beating out of my chest. Finally, she picks up.

"Hey, baby! I was wondering when I was going to hear from you again! How are you?"

"Hey ma, everything is fine. How are you?"

"NaTasha, I'm even better now that I'm hearing from you! But I wish you sounded a lot better. What's the matter?"

Mama always knew when something was up. There was a long awkward silence. "Hello? NaTasha, you still there?"

"Yes, Mama, I'm still here."

"Then tell me what's going on!"

"Mama, I can't hide this from you anymore. Aaron kicked the boys and me out of the house four months ago. He's filing for a divorce and plans on marrying another woman who he impregnated and has a child with. Corbin, Calvin, and I have been staying in an apartment, but we can only stay there for three more months before they start giving us eviction notices. Money is running low, and we're low on food. I have no job, and I'm pregnant with a baby girl. I'm not sure if I'm going to keep her. The thought of having Aaron's child after what he did kills me. I have a doctor's appointment in the morning, so we can talk about possibly...having...an...abortion."

There's a long pause, then I hear, "Alvin, we've got to go to New York! Our girl is in trouble."

"Mama? Mama?"

"Baby, we're going to catch the next flight to New York, and unless your appointment you have is for a check-up on the wellness of that sweet baby girl, you BETTER cancel it! If you abort that child, you'll surely regret it. You'll come to find that baby girl will be one of your greatest blessings."

"But Mama..."

"I MEAN IT! Unless it's for a check-up, CANCEL the appointment. I'll see you in a few hours."

"Okay, Mama."

"Your father is on the way to wire you some money. Honey, you've got to believe that God will take care of you. You WILL have joy again. You WILL smile again. You WILL love again. Take this time to get closer to God and strengthen your prayer life. You've got to stay encouraged. Those sweet babies need their mama."

All I could say was, "Yes, ma'am."

"We'll be there as soon as we can. I love you!"

"Love you too, Mama. I'm going to go get the boys from school."

Mama always knew how to make me feel better. I was so glad I called her after all.

"Hey, boys! How was your day?"

Corbin is silent. He hasn't been coping well with everything that has happened. He's been blaming himself for why his dad was no longer involved. Calvin starts talking about the things he did at daycare.

"That's wonderful, Calvin! Corbin, I know exactly what will cheer you up."

"What is it, Mommy?"

"Grandma and Grandpa are coming to visit, and they'll be staying with us for a while."

"Really?" Corbin asked.

"Well, I'm happy now that they are coming!"

"Me too."

We get back home, and I call my doctor's office to cancel my appointment. It feels like a weight has been lifted off me. I begin tidying up my room in preparation for my parents, and I can't help but feel relieved and thankful I made the phone call to my mom. We eat a quick supper, and I get the boys ready for bed. Now they are fast asleep, and I am wide awake in anticipation of my parents arriving within the next few hours.

I feel like I haven't slept at all, but I have to get the boys off to school and be ready to pick my parents up from the airport. I get the boys ready and drop them off. Within thirty minutes of dropping them off, I get a call from my mom that they are at the airport. I head to the airport, feeling a mixture of emotions: nervous, anxious, excited, and not fully knowing what to expect or what my parents are going to say when we see each other face-to-face. I arrive at the airport, and I finally see my parents. "Here goes nothin'," I said to myself.

"Hey, Mama! Hey, Daddy!"

They greet me and hug me tightly. We stood there for what seemed like an eternity, hugging each other and holding each other tightly. It's been a while since I've seen my parents face-to-face. I really needed this. I didn't want to let them go. How could I let myself get to this point? I just felt so empty inside. I needed love. I needed Jesus. I needed to be surrounded by the ones who loved me. I needed my parents. How could I have allowed myself to push everyone that loved me away in a time like this? Why would I allow myself to hurt and go through this pain alone? All these thoughts were racing through my mind as I was looking at the faces of my loving parents. The looks on their faces expressed concern, but mostly love.

It was about a thirty-minute drive from the airport to my apartment. The conversation was casual and flowed. There was no judgment. No condemnation. Now that I think about it, I'm not sure why I thought there would be. Part of me thought my parents would blame me for Aaron leaving. Maybe I thought this because I was blaming myself. There was none of that, and I was grateful.

We get to my apartment, I open the door, and my parents step inside. My dad stands in the living room, looking disturbed while my mom walks around, examining the place. There is an awkward silence; I mean, you could hear a pin drop. The first words my mom utters are, "I don't see why you need to continue staying here," my dad nods in agreement. "Being here will only remind you of what you think you lost; it will only remind you of what happened, which will not be good for you or my precious grandchildren," she examines my pregnant body. "You did cancel that appointment, right?"

"Yes, Mama, I canceled it."

"Good! That baby girl you are carrying has a special calling on her life, and she is going to be one of your greatest blessings. You will see that in due time."

My father chimes in, "What time do the boys get out of school?"

"At 2:15 p.m., Daddy."

"Okay, we will need to get their records transferred because you all are coming back to California with us. You're not staying here. We've already booked plane tickets for you all, so we'll just need to get some boxes to pack up your clothes and get them shipped."

All I could say was, okay. I mean, I didn't really have a choice, right? A few hours pass, and we have all our clothes boxed up, and we worked it out to where our clothes, along with my car, would be shipped to California. We head to the boys' school to handle all the paperwork to get their records transferred to California and to pick them up because we are flying out ASAP. My parents weren't playing any games. They were adamant we come back with them on the first thing smokin'. Once we got the boys in the car, my dad explained to them that we were moving.

Wow, this place has been my home for the last ten years. I didn't think I would be leaving New York City, at least not this way. As we were driving through the city, I couldn't help but reminisce about the good times I had there. Also, it was the only place my boys knew, so I did have some concerns about how they would adjust to a new environment. They are both vibrant little boys, so I was sure they would be fine. The question was, would I?

Late that night, we waited at the airport to board the plane. Next stop: California.

# Chapter 3
## *What's Next?*

Palm Springs, California. It's been forever since I've been home, and I felt a mixture of emotions. Part of me was relieved and excited to be home with my family. The other part was dreading it because I knew the news would travel soon about what happened between Aaron and me. My parents have a huge house in Palm Springs, my father is a pastor of a megachurch, and it's been forever since I've been there. I just know all those church people will be in my business, asking me about Aaron. I know I may sound negative, but I just know what's ahead of me, and I'm just not feeling it. I already feel bad enough about the situation as it is, and I just don't feel like the fakeness of people acting like they care, when I know they really don't. These types of people only want news, and I don't want my personal business and issues to be the "news" of the church or the town. I'm already trying to figure out how I'm going to explain it to my brothers and the rest of my family, but it's still early in the morning, so I have time to at least try to figure it out.

"What's on your mind?"

"Nothing, Mama," I said.

"That's a lie! Girl, when are you going to learn that I know you, so I know when you're being honest and when you're not?"

"Okay, Mama, here's the thing. I'm just under a lot of stress right now. I know you know, but it's just too much. Then I'm worried about how I'm going to tell everyone about it before they find out from the presses. Also, I know the church will be all up in my business. I'm just not feeling it, just not ready to deal with it."

"First of all, you're not going through anything alone. Have you forgotten about God? Have you forgotten He was the one with you and keeping you all this time? If you seek Him, He will tell you how to handle this, and He will give you the words to say. What about the church people? I don't know why you're so concerned about what they will think. Who cares what they think? It's none of their business, none of their concern. You have to believe and trust God! One minute you're up, the next minute you're down. Don't allow the enemy to toss you to and fro. A double-minded person is unstable in all their ways. You've got to stand firm and hold on to God and His word."

I couldn't say anything. I really was trying to soak in everything.

"Daughter, you need to get some rest. Once you've rested, we'll get started with finding you a new doctor and everything."

"Okay, Mama. I love you."

"Love you too, baby."

I tried to rest, but I couldn't. I couldn't help but think about Aaron and everything that happened. I couldn't help but think about the fact that I had two young boys who would never be able to understand why their father left them. I couldn't help but think about my baby girl on the way and how she, too, would never understand why he chooses not to be a part of her life. I couldn't help but think about how the man who was the love of my life abandoned me. Not only did he abandon me, but he also abandoned our family. He made vows to me that he chose not to keep. I couldn't help but think about how I was going through a divorce and how the man I loved cheated on me. With all of this on my mind, it was hard to rest. It was a lot to take in; it was a lot to deal with. I know I wasn't alone, but that's what I felt. I was hurt. I felt abandoned. This cannot be my life! I know I couldn't depend on my parents to take care of us forever, so I'm going to have to look for a job eventually.

I slept for three hours, but it felt like five minutes. I was exhausted. Mama said she found a doctor for me and was able to get me an appointment for the next morning. She also got the boys enrolled in school, and they could start tomorrow as well. Daddy said he had a job for me at the church because he's in need of a secretary.

"I don't know, Daddy, the church secretary. I haven't held a position in a church in forever."

"We'll show you the ropes. I know you'll get the hang of it, and I think you'd be the perfect fit."

"I don't know, Daddy."

"Listen, baby girl. I'd rather give you the position and pay you than someone else. Your mother told me you're worried about how the church people will respond. I understand your feelings, but you have nothing to worry about. The situation is really none of their concern. Baby girl, in time, you will see that this is going to work for your good, and you're going to be better off than you were before. Just trust God."

"I do, Daddy."

"Well, then you need to act like you trust Him. Folks who really trust God don't walk around moping with their head down. They walk with their heads up and a smile on their face because even though they can't physically see how the Lord is turning things around for them, they see it with their spiritual eyes, and they believe. Your mother and I can tell you that until we're blue in the face, and we can believe all we want to for you, but it all means nothing unless you believe it and trust God for yourself."

I know that my parents are trying to help and encourage me, but it just seems like they're preaching at me. My dad really wants me to take the position as secretary at the church. I could definitely use the money, but I'm a little skeptical about accepting it. I've held positions in the church before, and because I was a PK (preacher's kid), people weren't too fond of it because they felt like it kept their child from having an opportunity.

"Baby girl, have you made a decision yet?"

"I just don't know, Daddy."

"Well, I need you to know. I'll tell you what, why don't you come to the church with me. I can show you around and give you a rundown of everything that you'd be doing, and then you can decide. I know I can trust you, and I'd rather give you the job. I know you're planning on going back to school and all, so you'd be able to do the job at the church and still go to school. Just a little something to keep in mind, but you can make your decision once you've visited the church."

"Okay, Daddy, I'll visit the church with you."

"Great! We can go now."

We pull up to the church, and I'm just in awe at how huge and beautiful it is. The sanctuary is HUGE, and there are several classrooms for children of all age groups. I can already tell that Corbin and Calvin will really like it here. There were a lot of people at the church preparing for Sunday. As daddy was showing me around, something in my gut told me I needed to take the position at the church. Looking around, and just being in the building, felt like I was finally home. I hadn't stepped foot in a church in years. I let Aaron talk me into worshipping at home, which just turned into sleeping in super late on Sundays and watching the games that came on TV. I felt the presence of the Lord for the first time in a long time, and all I was doing was touring the church building! No wonder I've been feeling the way I have because God never left me, I left him. My heart was filled with remorse, and I was very repentant. I was so overwhelmed by the presence of God that I began to weep.

"Is everything alright, baby girl?"
"Daddy, I'm home! I'm where I'm supposed to be. I will take the position as the church secretary."

# Chapter 4
## *Home*

I can't shake the feeling that I had the other day at the church. I can't believe I left my first love: God. I can't believe I allowed some man to lead me away from my Heavenly Father. Maybe this is the reason why everything happened the way it did. Maybe this was God's way of bringing me back to Him because He knew I was at my lowest and had nowhere to fall but on my knees. I'm not gonna lie, it still hurt Aaron left, and in the manner he did, but I couldn't allow myself to be bitter; I wouldn't allow myself to be bitter. I will take this time to find the real NaTasha because she's lost herself. She conformed to the woman that she thought others wanted her to be and forsook who she really was to fit in. By forsaking herself, she forsook God. She turned her back on Him. This ends tuhday! The real NaTasha knows her identity is hidden in Christ. She needs God! She will do everything possible to get closer and deeper in Him, for He has given her newfound strength.

# Chapter 5
# Family

Daddy and I were out running errands for Mama. When we returned home, we found all my brothers were there. Did I mention I have five brothers? Alvin Jr. (AJ), Travis, Scott, Darrell, and Trey. I am the only girl and the youngest. I'm not sure if Mama told them I'm back home, but if she did, I know she didn't tell them why because Mama's not one to tell someone else's business. I'm going to have to tell them everything, and the thought of that terrifies me because they are all crazy! When I say crazy, I mean C R A Z Y, especially when it comes to their little sister. AJ wanted to fight Aaron for "dragging me across the country" when we first got married. I can only imagine what he's going to want to do to him once he finds out all that's happened. As I walk into the living room with Daddy, all of them look surprised, yet happy to see me, and they immediately jumped up from the couch to greet me.

"Tasha, you ain't tell nobody you were comin' to town! Mama and Pop ain't say nothin' either," AJ said as he hugged me.

"How long you been here?" Travis chimed in.

"About two days," I said.

"Two days? And you ain't bother letting us know you were here?" said Scott.

"Y'all chill. Maybe the girl was tired and just trying to settle in. I'm sure she was going to let us know sooner or later."

Darrell is always defending me and coming to my rescue. I can always count on him to be the voice of reason that calms my other brothers down. Trey was very impatient as he awaited my answers, then he said, "Aaron could've at least told us y'all would be here. Congratulations on baby number three, but where's my brother-in-law, and where are my nephews? We ain't seen y'all in forever!"

Ahhh, here it goes... "Well, first of all, it's good to see y'all too. I didn't tell you all I was coming because it was urgent that we, me and the boys, get here immediately."

"Urgent?" said AJ.

"Yes, urgent. Aaron didn't tell you anything because he and I are no longer together, and he doesn't know, nor do I think he cares that the boys and I are here."

"What do you mean y'all ain't together? Y'all been rockin' with each other forever. What happened?" asked Scott.

"Before I say another word, all of you need to sit down."

They proceeded to sit down on the couch. "Aaron left me to be with his mistress, a woman he was seeing for the past seven years. He has a son with her that's the same age as Corbin, and she's pregnant by him too. I had no idea of their existence until the day he kicked the boys and me out four months ago. He's filed for divorce, and we go to court in two months. It's been a hard four months being a pregnant single mom with no work experience or college degree. It's been difficult for the boys, especially Corbin, because they can't understand why their father would leave them, and I can't either. He took everything we knew and loved and gave it to some trash that's probably gonna take him for everything he's got."

"Wait, hold the phone. This happened four months ago? FOUR months ago? Are you serious Tasha? Why didn't you tell us about it then? Why didn't you call us? We would've handled that coward!" Scott said.

"Pride. Pride wouldn't let me tell anyone what was really going on. Pride wanted me to make you all think and believe everything was okay. Pride wanted me to think I could handle it on my own until reality came crashing in. I hit rock bottom and had no one to call on but God and family. This is why we're here, and quite frankly, I'm glad to be here."

A few months ago, I didn't think I would be here.

After letting that off my chest, I felt even more relief than when I told it to Mama and Daddy the first time. That quickly turned to worry once I saw the crazed, angry, yet hurt look on AJ's face.

"No. no. No, no, NO! This is NOT okay. He can't do that to you. He can't do that to Corbin and Calvin. He can't do that to his unborn baby. He ain't a man. No REAL man would do that to his wife and kids—a pregnant wife at that. I'm gone handle him. I'm gone handle him. Better yet, Imma kill him!"

AJ raged as he paced back and forth. I could even hear him cursing underneath his breath.

"Boy, if you don't stop all that cursing and foolishness in my house! This is holy ground," Daddy yelled. "Get a grip on yourself, boy! 'Vengeance is mine. I will repay' saith the Lord in Romans 12:19. Go act like a fool if you want to; you'll mess around and get locked up! All that anger does damage to your soul, and I tell you son, ain't nobody worth me going to hell over. I know Tasha is your baby sister, and you want to do everything in your power to protect her, but you've got to get a grip on yourselves. This whole situation has taken a toll on her and the boys. They need our love and support to get through this. They don't need anybody acting like fools tryna hurt people. What kind of example would that set for her boys? Huh, what kind of example would that set for your nephews? You wouldn't be any better than Aaron in my book carrying on like that."

"Pop, I know you're a preacher and all, but are you for real? You ain't even angry at what that chump did to your daughter and grandkids?" asked Trey.

"Boy, of course, I am! You think I don't have no feelings? The Bible tells us to be angry, but sin not. That means I can feel what I'm feeling but not act upon it. All I can do is pray for Tasha, her boys and pray for Aaron to see his ways and how it's destroyed his family. God can do more with situations and people than we can."

"Ain't that the truth," Mama chimed in.

# Chapter 6
## *The Moment of Truth*

I never thought I would be in divorce court, but I came to terms with it. My parents and I flew back to New York for court. After six months, I felt like I was finally at peace with the whole situation. Yeah, it hurt, but I could not and would not force a relationship, nor would I be with someone who disrespected me and didn't treat me like the queen that I am. I don't know how I didn't see any of this coming, but everything happens for a reason, right?

Aaron hasn't seen or spoken to his sons in six months. I'm not sure how this court session is going to go, but I do know I want and intend to get full custody of our boys. He hasn't bothered to do anything for them in the time we've been apart, so I am certain he has no intention to do anything once we're divorced. With the help of God and the support of my family, we really don't need anything from him; however, I will ensure to make him pay child support for his sons whom he has chosen to neglect, and his unborn daughter who will never know him or have a relationship with him. It breaks my heart for my kids, but I pray they know none of this is their fault. I hope they are able to forgive their dad someday, and I hope they will be able to move on and not harbor any hate in their hearts towards him or his other kids. Arriving in New York certainly uncovered all these fresh wounds.

## Court Day

Well, here it is, the moment of truth: court day. I walked into the room with my parents and the attorney they hired for me. On the other side of the room, I see Aaron, his concubine, and his attorney. Aaron looks old and haggard. He looked nothing like the Aaron I once knew and loved. My attorney presented my case, and I was able to speak before the judge. It became Aaron's turn, and I thought he was going to make up a bunch of lies, but he was truthful. He was honest about his infidelity and negligence of our children.

"Yes, I cheated on her for seven years. Yes, I have a child with my soon-to-be new wife and a child on the way. Yes, I have a child on the way with my soon-to-be ex-wife, but that was a mistake. I am no longer in love with NaTasha, and I want no dealings with any parts of her. I think it would be best for her to have custody of the kids we have together. I have a new woman and new responsibilities. I just want to be free of NaTasha and move on with my life, and I'm sure she wants to move on as well. I'll pay the child support and the alimony, whatever it is I need to do, but please, just let me move on with the woman that I am in love with," Aaron said.

The judge was astounded at the words that came out of his mouth. I was surprised as well. Aaron's concubine didn't like the part about him saying he would pay alimony and child support, though! The judge did just what Aaron requested. He granted our divorce, but Aaron was required to pay me one million dollars in alimony. ONE MILLION DOLLARS. I was not looking for that at all! Did I mention he had to pay child support on top of that? It's because he had the means to do it being a well-known author and playwright. Once we were dismissed, Aaron didn't look my way. His concubine was furious at the amount he had to pay. Well, I guess that puts a downer on their new wedding plans. News had already hit in New York he and I were divorced before it actually happened and was all the gossip. I thought I would feel some type of way about it, but there was nothing I could do. I fulfilled my duties as a wife and mother, and that's all I could do. I loved Aaron, but that wasn't good enough. He was now legally free to do whatever he pleased. I was now legally free, and could finally move on and help my children cope with his decision.

My priority was my children. I will ensure they have the best life possible. I thanked God for carrying me even when I didn't know I needed to be carried. I thanked God for bringing me back to Him. I thanked God that even though I didn't fully understand everything that took place, and I didn't know what was going to happen next, I could rest assured He had me. I thanked Him for giving me loving parents that would always have my back and support me. I thanked God for my crazy brothers too (I am glad they did not make the trip with us for court), for although they may be wild, they have my best interest at heart. I thanked God for my two young kings and my unborn queen. God knew what He was doing when He gave them to me. I thanked God for being God and for freeing me both spiritually, mentally, and physically through this situation. I could move on now because I WAS FREE.

# Chapter 7
## *Hope*

It feels good to say that I'm finally able to put all of the drama with Aaron behind me and move on with my life. God has been better than good to me! I've learned to count it all joy. I've even been excited about my baby girl's arrival; she could come any day now. I'm on bed rest, but I've been getting everything ready for her arrival, and I can actually say I'm excited to be birthing a daughter; I'm excited to be birthing a woman of God. Although she is still in my womb, I can tell there is something peculiar about her. She's already been set apart by God, and she's going to do marvelous works for His kingdom. It's an honor to be able to carry a young queen who will do mighty things for the kingdom of God.

My boys seem to be coping with the situation well. They really like their new school, church, and their teachers. They are flourishing in this new environment. They are both a breath of fresh air. It's amazing to see how well they were able to bounce back and become the vibrant boys I knew them to be. I know they still have their concerns about their father's whereabouts, and I know that will never change because their father will always be a part of their memory. I pray they remember the good things about him and not the bad, for his sake.

I was packing baby girl's diaper bag and my hospital bag when I felt a sharp pain in my stomach and noticed that my water broke.

"Ma!" I said.

"Yes, baby?" Mama said.

"We need to get to the hospital, my water just broke, and I felt a sharp pain in my stomach."

"Okay, baby! I'll grab your things; you just get in the car!"

Throughout the car ride, I'm not sure who was more nervous: my parents or me. They were frantic while trying to keep me calm when they weren't remaining calm themselves. My contractions were getting closer and closer, but thank God we made it to the hospital in time!

On October 10, 1999, at 1:00 p.m., Taylor Gabrielle Campbell was born. She was the most perfect, most beautiful baby girl I'd ever seen. Despite everything we'd been through, I had so much hope looking at her beautiful little face. I was so overwhelmed with joy and emotions that when I saw her, I wept. "Mommy is so happy that you are finally here! You are so beautiful, and

Mommy loves you so much. I can't wait for you to meet your brothers," I told her.

They took her away from me to clean her up and make sure everything was well with her. She was perfect! I birthed a healthy baby girl, and all glory goes to God. She was eight pounds and eight ounces; did I mention she was absolutely perfect? It was an all-natural birth, no epidural, for she came rather quickly.

My brothers came and brought the boys to meet their baby sister, and they were in love. They were in absolute awe over their baby sister. It was amazing and beautiful to see. I hope when they grow up, they'll remain close, love one another, look out for each other, and protect each other. I pray they will have an unbreakable bond. And even when they have disagreements or arguments, I pray they go right back to lovin' each other. I believe all my children have a special calling on them, and I pray I am able to nurture them for their callings. I know they will all do amazing things.

# Chapter 8
## *A Fresh Start?*

It's been a year since I've moved back home, been working at the church, and since I've had Taylor. A childhood friend has been trying to get close to me. His name is Tyler Washington. He's thirty-two, single, wealthy, and has no children. We grew up in the same church, and he was pretty close with my brothers, so I saw him often, but I was never interested in him (and I'm still not). It's been a year since my divorce, and I never even thought of the possibility of another relationship. The only relationship I'm focused on is my relationship with God. I vowed to focus on my relationship with God, nurture my children, finish school, and move out of my parents' house. Dating is the farthest thing from my mind right now.

"You're sweet, but I can't go out with you, Tyler."

"May I ask why?" Tyler said.

"I've just got a lot going on with school, here at the church, and my kids. I don't see how a relationship would play into all of that right now," I said.

"I see," he said.

"Look, you're a great guy, and any woman would be lucky, blessed, to have you. Why are you interested in me? Why do you want a woman who's already been divorced and has three kids? Don't you want someone like you who's never been touched?" I asked.

He gazed into my eyes and said, "I want you. It's different when I'm around you. I know in my heart you are the one God wants me to be with. I knew I wanted to be with you when we were younger, but you were with Aaron, and I didn't say anything. I can't go back in the past, but we're here now. We're both here now, and all I'm asking for is a chance. Just give me a chance to love you the way that you're supposed to be loved. Until then, I'll continue to pursue you like Christ pursues and loves His church. I love you NaTasha Campbell. I'm in love with you, and your children are a blessing. I'd count it an honor and a privilege to be a part of their lives."

I'm pretty sure I felt my jaw drop at his remarks. I was speechless. Here he is a tall, dark, handsome, SAVED man pouring out his heart to me after I rejected him. Can't he see I'm just not ready for another relationship?

"Tyler, my first marriage failed. I don't want to see that happen again. I don't want to feel that pain again. I don't think I'm ready. I don't think I'm ready for another relationship. I just need some time to pray and think about it."

"Okay," he said, "Take all the time you need. I'll be right here waiting."

I've seen Tyler at church, and he hasn't asked me anymore about our last conversation. I guess he's really giving me the time I said I needed. The crazy thing about it is now I can't stop thinking about him! What's going on, Lord? I thought once you get divorced, you couldn't marry again. I thought that because I was a young divorcee with three kids, no one would even want me. I thought I was damaged goods, so no one would even consider looking at me. I guess Tyler sees it differently. I guess Tyler sees me how God sees me: fearfully and wonderfully made. He thinks better of me than I do of myself. I'm in shock! I'm in awe! I don't really know what to think right now. The best thing to do is to go in my prayer closet.

*Lord, I'm so confused right now. Tyler is an amazing guy, but why me? I don't think that I'm ready for another relationship. I mean, it's only* been a year since I got divorced, and personally, I think I need to focus on raising my small children and finishing school. I still have hopes and dreams I want to accomplish with your help, of course, and I really don't want any distractions prohibiting that. Lord, I guess I'm asking if it's Your will for Tyler and me to be together? I mean, I detested the idea of a relationship, and I wasn't even interested in him until now. Now it seems like something's different, and I can't put my finger on it. Now, he's all I think about, besides You and the kids, of course. But then there's that too God: the kids. I don't want them getting attached to a man, and then things not work out. I know You freed me from my past, but Lord, I need Your help. I need Your wisdom in what to do. Lord, please give me clarity. In Jesus' name, I pray. Amen.

Instantly I heard God say, *Although Tyler is a wonderful man of God, he'd only be a distraction at this moment. My answer is not yet. You are just now coming back to me; you need to focus on your relationship with me, healing, and raising your children. You need to be clear so that you will be able to hear My voice and listen for My instructions. This may not make any sense right now, but you'll soon see the very man who hurt you will need your help. You still have unforgiveness and bitterness in your heart that you need to let go of; you need to let Me free you of this so you can then free others. Free people, free people. Don't worry about responding to Tyler at this moment; I will handle it so you both will be able to move on. Now daughter, take heed to My words.*

I didn't expect God to answer me so quickly! And part of it wasn't the answer that I was looking for. Part of me was relieved when God said not yet about Tyler and me being together, but the other part of me was saddened by it. I had no idea I still held unforgiveness and bitterness in my heart. I thought I was rid of all of that!? Well, God knows me better than I know myself, and He can see the deep, dark places of our hearts and souls. What really got me was the fact that God said the very man who hurt me would need my help. Let me think: Aaron?! What could Aaron possibly want and need from me? And after everything he's done to my family and me, why would I need to be the one to give it to him?

Then it happened. After pondering over what God had said, I turned on the television to see "BREAKING NEWS. Playwright and author Aaron Campbell has been admitted to a New

York hospital and has been diagnosed with a terminal illness. His status or condition has not yet been determined."

What in the world? I mean, what the what?! A terminal illness?! Lord, how could this be? I despised the man for what he did to the kids and me, but I never wanted anything bad like this to happen to him. Is this what you meant when You said he'd need my help, Lord? Like, my prayers? I'll certainly keep him in my prayers.

# Chapter 9
## *Answers*

God told me something I didn't necessarily want to hear. He said, "Go back to New York and visit Aaron in the hospital. They are labeling it a terminal illness, but it's not. With My help, only you can put a stop to what's really happening."

"Lord, what do You mean?"

"When you get there, you'll see. I'll make sure you see and know exactly what I'm talking about."

"Okay, God, if You say so, then I'll do it."

My parents were not thrilled I was going back to New York. "God told me to go visit him. I would not be doing this if He didn't tell me to," I said.

"Well, you're not going alone!" Daddy said.

"One of your brothers will go with you," Mama chimed in. "Darrell will go with you."

I was glad they chose Darrell. No disrespect to my other brothers, but Darrell was the most reasonable, sensible, and understanding brother out of all of them. He wasn't too thrilled about it either.

"I mean, I'm not trying to question God or anything, but I really don't understand. It's not a terminal illness? So, like someone's sabotaging him?" he asked.

"I don't know all of the ins and outs of it, but God said it's definitely not a terminal illness. He said once I got there, I would see and know what He's talking about. It's really urgent, so we have to get there immediately. Believe me, brother, I'm the last person that wants to go, but God said it, so that means it's a must that I go."

"Alright, little sister, I got your back, and I know God's got us. Let's do it."

Two days later, we arrived in New York. It didn't take us long to figure out where Aaron was because there were numerous paparazzi camped out in front of the hospital doors. I began to feel really bad for him. I couldn't imagine what he was going through—suffering while the whole world is waiting for your demise. Tragic! They were only letting relatives go into his hospital room.

"I'm his ex-wife," I said.

"I'm sorry, ma'am, but only relatives and people his wife determines may enter his hospital room," the nurse said.

Well, that sucks! "Lord, how am I supposed to help him and accomplish what You set out for me to do if I can't enter his room?"

"You don't need to enter his room to understand why you're there or how you're going to help him," God said.

I've never been so confused, but I'll trust Him and take Him at his word. We returned the next day. "Lil' sis, they're just going to tell us the same thing they told us yesterday, but I'm with you."

"We may have had some minor setbacks, but I know God spoke to me, so He'll work something out."

When we walked onto his hall, there was a new staff of nurses and doctors. His nurse recognized me as being his former wife, so she let Darrell and me into the room. I've never seen Aaron down like this before. He was resting, or maybe unconscious. Immediately, I heard God say, "Observe him closely. Look at everything about him and do it quickly for time is running out."

I looked at his face and noticed that he aged a little. I kept observing him, and something odd struck me about his IV and his arm.

"Sis, something's not right with his IV. There's no way he should look like that!" Darrell said.

We were in there for less than two minutes and picked up on that. How could the nurses not notice this? I immediately paged for a nurse to come in. After about five minutes, one finally came. "Is everything okay? How can I be of assistance?" the nurse said.

"Something's not right with his IV bag; it's discolored. Whatever it is, it's causing his whole body to turn, especially his arm," I said.

The nurse quickly turned her attention to what I was saying. "Oh my!" she gasped. She immediately called for other doctors and nurses to come into the room. They rushed Aaron out of the room and thanked us for bringing it to their attention. We were instructed to go into the waiting room.

"Do you think he was poisoned?" I asked Darrell.

"Ain't no doubt about it," Darrell said.

"But who? Who would want to hurt him?" I asked. Then it all made sense! Aaron was on a floor by himself because they weren't able to figure out what was wrong with him, and they feared his illness would spread to other patients. I saw Felicia and a strange man enter the room Aaron was in.

"Take out your phone and record their conversation. Make sure you get both of them in the video," God said.

I took out my phone as instructed, and I made sure they didn't see Darrell or me.

"He's not in here," Felicia said. "Do you think he finally kicked the can, and our plan worked?" she asked.

"There's no telling, but I'm sure of it 'cause not one of them nurses or doctors is on this hall! I must say, they were some dumb ones too because they ain't even notice he was being poisoned on their watch!" the man said.

"Shhhh...lower your voice! You don't want none of them to come back and hear us," Felicia said.

"But we did it, baby. We got rid of him once and for all! Now you, me, and the boys can live a lavish life at this idiot's expense. Our plan worked. We finally got rid of him, and now we can live the happy life we deserve!" the man said.

I accidentally let out a gasp, and they heard me. Darrell and I quickly hid behind the nurse's desk.

"What was that?" asked Felicia.

"Ain't nothin' baby," the man said.

"No, I know I heard someone," she said. "Who's there?!"

We didn't say a word. We waited for them to go back into the room, and then we hurried down the hall. We bolted down the stairs and hurried to the hospital's security office.

"One of your patients has been poisoned by his wife! It was deemed as a terminal illness, but it's not. He's being poisoned. You have to do something!" I was sobbing uncontrollably.

"Ma'am, please calm down so I can fully understand what you're saying," the officer said.

"Sir, we have video evidence to prove it," Darrell said as he showed the officer the video.

"Oh, my God!" the officer screamed as he called for backup.

"Hurry!" I said, "They should still be up there."

He also alerted Aaron's nurses and doctors of the real issue, but with many tests, they'd already made the discovery. We walked back to

Aaron's room with the officers a way off behind us.

"Well, well, well. What are you doing here?" Felicia asked.

"How could you do such a thing?" I asked.

"Why, whatever do you mean?" Felicia asked.

"Don't play dumb with me. I know what you did to Aaron," I said.

She began to laugh wickedly with the man beside her. "Oh, hush. Aaron didn't want you anyway, so I don't know why you're so concerned about him. Yes, I poisoned him. So what? I just wanted him to fall in love with me, believe that my kids were his, marry him, kill him off, and get rid of him so that I and my real love could live a happy life."

"You two are scums of the earth! How could you be so wicked?" I said.

"Oh now, now, dear. You know too much. Now we'll have to get rid of you too."

I signaled for the officers, and they ambushed those two heathens.

"You two are under arrest!" the officers yelled.

"You can't arrest us! You don't have proof of anything," Felicia screamed as she was being handcuffed.

"Is she being for real? You just admitted to everything, and your DNA is all over the patient. You both will be going away for a really long time," the officer responded.

I felt relief as I watched Felicia and her evil beau be handcuffed and escorted out of the hospital. Now I know why I was sent there and how I was supposed to help. Everything God told me made perfect sense now.

"I'm proud of you, sis. You were really brave," Darrell said.

"Brave? I was shaking in my boots, but God kept me together. God gets the glory for all of this," I said.

It didn't take long for all of what happened to reach the news. Darrell and I were called heroes. I never wanted any of this, the publicity, I just wanted to do what God wanted me to do. I was informed they were able to get most, if not all, the poison out of Aaron's system. The only thing left for him to do was recover.

# Chapter 10
## *Recovery*

We were in the waiting room for hours. I just needed to know Aaron would be okay so I could head back home. God had really done a work in me because most women would not endure all that, especially after what Aaron put me through. Nonetheless, I was glad I was obedient to God, and I hoped Aaron would have a change of heart and really seek after God.

We got notice Aaron was in his recovery room, and we could go see him. Darrell and I walked into his room, and he was not happy to see us. I can't say I didn't expect this response from him.

"Why are you two here? Where's my wife?" he said.

"Well, hello to you too. We fly halfway across the world to visit Lil' ole you, and this is the response we get? The disrespect," Darrell said.

"I'm sorry...thank you all for coming? It's not like we're on good terms with each other...anyway...where is my wife?" Aaron asked.

I remained silent. I couldn't believe the very man whose life God just saved was acting this way. He then got even more annoyed with us and turned on the TV to see his wife on BREAKING NEWS: Wife attempts to poison Aaron Campbell and ex-wife helps to save him. "WHAT?!" Aaron yelled.

"Nah, nah, nah! That can't be true! Felicia loves me, and she'd never do anything like that!" Aaron screamed.

"Are you kidding me?" Darrell asked. "Bro, the girl doesn't love you! She tried to kill you! Oh, and them kids you thought were yours, ain't yours either," Darrell said.

"Aaron, you don't need to worry about all of that right now. You just need to focus on healing and getting better so you can get out of here," I said.

"Oh, best believe I'll get better and get out of here...and I don't need you to do it!" Aaron said.

"Are you telling me the very woman that I loved, the woman that I left you for tried to kill me? She just wanted me for my money? And the kids aren't mine?" Aaron asked me.

I was taken aback by his rude demeanor, and it took every bit of Jesus, and I mean EVERY bit of Jesus in me to remain calm when talking to him.

"Are you serious right now? You just had a near-death experience, and you're in here screaming at my brother and me like we're the ones who tried to kill you when all we're trying to do is help you. Yes, it's true about Felicia. She was using you the entire time and only wanted your money. I'm sorry, but her kids were not yours. In fact, they were the offspring of the man she schemed with to plan your demise. I know it hurts, and believe me, no one gets it more than I do. But, if I were you, I'd be thanking and praising God that He chose to save my life! He chose to rescue you, and He really didn't have to. God has given you a second chance at life, but what you do with it is on you. You're worried about some kids whom you THOUGHT were yours when you have kids that ARE yours. And all I'm going to say is that YOUR kids need their father," I said.

Aaron looked puzzled and then smiled weirdly at me. "NaTasha, I get it, and I'm sorry but...there's no getting back together. I understand you're still in love with me, and I appreciate all of your help. Yes, I understand my kids do need me. Maybe we could co-parent and work out a schedule, but as far as us? There is no us, okay?" Aaron said.

"Bro.... you've got to be kidding me. Sis...is he for real?" Darrell asked.

I felt like banging my head against the wall. "Lord, is my work here done? Please tell me my assignment is done before I put this fool back in ICU!" I said. "Aaron, it's clear that you're still high and doped up on whatever Felicia has been putting in your system. We're going to leave and come back tomorrow. Hopefully, you'll be in your right mind, have some sense, and then maybe we could really have a sensible conversation. Because this ain't it," I said as Darrell, and I walked out of the door.

"Can you believe that jack-behind?" Darrell asked.

"I don't want to talk about it. Let's just grab some dinner and head back to the room. I'm exhausted, and I'm sure you are too," I said.

"Word," Darrell said.

We ate dinner, and I took a moment to take in everything that just happened and unwind. *God, this is not the way I expected things to go. I thought Aaron would be happy Darrell and I came to help save him. If You didn't send us here, he'd be a goner. Surely this is not how things are supposed to end for him. Lord, please prick his heart so that he would know that You were the One who saved his life, and You're the One who's keeping him. Lord save Aaron's soul. I don't want him to perish. I don't want him to die and go to hell when he doesn't have to. Please, Lord, save him and clean him up. In Jesus' name. Amen.*

The next morning, we returned to the hospital to visit Aaron once again. I prayed for him that previous night, and I know God heard me. Aaron's demeanor was very different this time.

"Good morning, y'all. I'm sorry for how I acted with you yesterday. I was hurt to find out via TV all Felicia had done to me, but that was no reason for me to lash out on the two of you. You guys were only trying to help. My nurses and doctors told me all you guys did for me. THANK YOU! Thank you both, for if it weren't for you two, I'd be a dead man right now, and a woman who didn't love me would be livin' it up with a scum at my expense. I suppose I also have God to thank for that because He's really the One that saved my life. He speaks, and things happen. I'm not sure why He chose to rescue me, but I'm thankful that He did. Darrell, I appreciate you coming here with NaTasha. And NaTasha, I'm sorry for everything! I'm sorry for hurting both you and the kids. You deserve to be with someone that loves and adores you and who will treat you with the respect you deserve. You're a true gem, and it's too bad it took me until now to figure that out. Thanks for everything that you've done for our kids. They are really lucky to have you as their mother," Aaron said.

Wow! I didn't know what to say to him. "Wow, Aaron. I'm literally speechless right now," I said.

"It's been a long time coming, and it's way overdue, but I truly am sorry. I know my words can't undo or fix anything, but please know I truly am sorry. Also, how are the kids? I know we have a daughter, what's her name?" Aaron asked.

Now he's talking' right. "Corbin and Calvin miss you. Some days they're okay with you not being there for them, and other days they are not. But they are thriving in school and are really a breath of fresh air. Yes, our daughter is now a year old, and her name is Taylor Gabrielle. She brings so much joy to my life and to everyone around her. I'm sure she'd love to meet her daddy," I said.

"I miss the boys as well, and I promise as soon as I'm able, I will see them, apologize, and explain everything to them. I should have never left them in the first place," Aaron said.

He also mumbled something else, and I'm not certain, but it sounded like he said, "I should have never left you."

"Wow. Taylor Gabrielle. That's a beautiful name, and I'm sure she's a beautiful little girl," Aaron said.

"She sure is! Beautiful, just like her mama!" Darrell chimed in.

I must say I was pleased with where the conversation was going.

"I know you guys have an early morning flight tomorrow, but could you do me this one favor?" Aaron asked.

"Of course, what is it?" I asked.

"I want to be saved! Will you pray for me?" Aaron asked

"Of course! If you believe in your heart that Jesus died on the cross for your sins and accept Him as your Lord and Savior, He will save you! *Father God, thank you for Aaron's decision. Thank you for pricking his heart to want to be saved. He believes and confesses that JESUS IS LORD! He understands Jesus died on the cross to save him of his sins, and he has accepted Jesus' free gift of salvation. We ask You to come into his heart right now, Father, save his soul, and make him whole. Fill him with your precious Holy Spirit and let him know he is free of ALL sin, guilt, and shame. We thank you for his new life and salvation. In Jesus' name. Amen."*

We exchanged telephone numbers so he could chat with the kids and eventually schedule visits when he was able to. My, oh my, how God had blown my mind! He truly is the Master Potter, who is more than able to put broken pieces back together again. I was excited about Aaron's new journey in the faith of our Lord and Savior Jesus Christ. I was ecstatic he wants to reconnect with our kids, and we'll all be able to heal. Now, let the healing begin.

# Chapter 11
## *Healing*

It had been about two months since Darrell and I visited Aaron in the hospital, and he hadn't called the kids yet. I know no one can change overnight, but I honestly thought he'd turned over a new leaf with him getting saved and all (or at least I thought he got saved). I thought he meant what he said when he talked about reaching out to the kids and re-establishing a relationship with them. I thought he would make good on his promise and allow the boys to get the true healing they needed. I battled with this because I hated seeing my kids sad because they missed their dad. It didn't really affect Taylor because she never knew him, but it took a huge toll on Corbin and Calvin.

     With all of this in mind, I decided to do the unthinkable. I decided to call Aaron. We did exchange phone numbers, and the phone works both ways, right? I mean, if he's not going to call, then I guess I need to be the one to do so, right? I decided I would see what's really up and find out if he actually intended to make good on his promise concerning the kids. I dialed the number he gave me, and the phone rang for what seemed like forever before going to his voicemail. The message said, "You've reached Aaron Campbell. You know what to do, just leave me a message after the beep, and I'll get back to you as soon as possible." I debated on whether or not to leave a message or to try calling again later. Ultimately, I decided to leave a message, but Lord, what do I say? "Hi Aaron, it's NaTasha. I hope you're doing well. Please call me back at your earliest convenience. Bye."

Why was I trippin' about giving him a call and leaving a voice message? Was I nervous that he would actually pick up? Or was I nervous because I thought he was back to his old ways? I never know what's going to come out of his mouth, so that's probably what that was. Or could it be....NO! No, no, no! There's ABSOLUTELY NO WAY I could possibly still be in lo.... I don't even want to say it! I don't want to think about it either because the possibility of us getting back together is slim to none! I'd be out of my mind to want to get back together with him after all of the foolery I've endured! No, I know what it is. I'm not in love with him; I just have compassion for him. Whew! That's good to know, and it's actually great to know that I do actually have compassion for him because there was a time I didn't. That in itself shows growth and healing!

I pushed all the foolery out of my mind and went to fulfill my duties at the church. The church people got wind that Darrell and I went to visit Aaron in the hospital and how we helped save his life. Some of them were calling us heroes, while others thought I was nuts to go. Tyler was among the few that thought it was questionable I went. I tried explaining it was the Lord who sent me there, and I didn't do it on my own merit. Some understood, and some didn't, but I really didn't care. I guess the thing that confused me the most was the fact that these were church people. CHURCH PEOPLE, who are supposed to KNOW God, show love, and be compassionate for God's people. I wondered how these people could be judging me for doing a noble act that GOD COMMANDED me to do. I was slightly irritated with them, but did my best not to show it.

Tyler, along with a few others, were around when my phone rang. It was Aaron calling me back, so I headed back to my office to take his call when I heard, "See Tyler, I told you she was still in love with that man! I don't know why you'd wanna waste your time with her anyway. After all, she does have THREE kids."

It was Rhonda who worked in the children's ministry. I turned around and looked at her. I was getting ready to defend myself when I heard God say, "I will fight for you. You don't need to say anything in response to her. You're not battling with flesh and blood but with evil spirits and principalities in heavenly places. She wants to get a rise out of you. Don't give her that satisfaction. Be strong and encouraged for I, The Lord, am fighting for you."

So, I didn't say anything and proceeded to go to my office. Rhonda looked shocked I didn't say anything. Tyler looked hurt and confused. Rhonda, seeing Tyler's facial expression, had a smirk on her face.

I picked up the phone, "Hello?" I said.

"Hey, it's Aaron. I was just giving you a callback," he said.

"Yeah, we haven't spoken since you were in the hospital, so I figured I'd call to check on you," I said.

"Oh, that's nice of you because you really didn't have to," he said. "Yeah, well, I just wanted to see how you were doing," I said.

"Well, you know I almost died, and all 'cause my wife tried to kill me...so, just trying to cope with that whole situation...along with the legal things that come with filing for a divorce and all...honestly never thought I'd be divorced twice, well the first one was my fault. I guess I'm saying I'm just happy to be here," he said.

"You're a blessed one...not many people survive what you survived. God is faithful even when we aren't," I said.

"Yeah...He sure is. I'm grateful God sent you and Darrell there to help save me, both in the natural and the spiritual realm. I'm still trying to figure this thing out; I'm still trying to figure out this new life with God. I was on my way to hell and didn't know it. I thought I was just livin' life ya know? But that's not the life at all. Cheating, lying, all of that is not it. Again, I can never tell you enough. I truly am sorry."

"Aaron, you don't have to..."

"No, I really do. And I meant what I said about contacting the kids. I've been meaning to call, but all of the craziness here has consumed my time," he said.

There was a long awkward silence. "Hello? NaTasha? You still there?" Aaron asked.

"I'm here," I said.

"But yeah, like I was saying, I'd love to talk to the kids...and even visit with them if that's okay with you."

"I know they'd love to hear from you, so that's cool," I said.

The kids were at the church with me. My mom brought them into my office so they could speak with their dad. Corbin wanted to talk first.

"Dad? Dad? Is it really you?" he said.

"Hey, Corbin! How are…"

"Dad, why'd you leave? I miss you! Calvin misses you! I don't know if Taylor even knows you! You missed my birthday, you know," Corbin said.

"Son…I'm so sorry. I should have never left you, Calvin, or Taylor. I promise I am going to spend the rest of my life making it up to you, your brother, and your sister," Aaron said.

"What about mom?" Corbin asked. "How are you going to make it up to her?"

My face turned red, but I thought it was cute that he even asked.

"Well, son, how do you think I could make it up to her?" Aaron asked.

"You could buy her some flowers or candy, or you could just buy me toys.

Yeah, the toys, she would like that."

Really Corbin, REALLY? But that cracked me up! Calvin was next to talk, and since he heard his brother mention toys, that's ALL he wanted to talk about. Taylor, on the other hand, was all giggly and talking gibberish lol. This all brought joy to my heart. What a difference a year can make! I'm just glad my kids were finally able to speak with their father, and I'm glad Aaron was actually acting like their father. It came time for me to close out the conversation.

"Okay, Aaron..."
"Actually, NaTasha, I have a question," he said.
"Okay, what is it?" I asked.
"Would you ever consider moving back to New York?" Aaron asked.

Why would I move back to New York? Yeah, he would be able to see the kids, but there are too many wounds there, and his family was still not speaking to me. So, unless God said otherwise, it's a no for me. "Actually...no...I really like it here in California, and I think the kids like it here too," I said.
"Okay," he said. "Then my only other option would be to move to California so I can be closer to the kids and see them on a regular basis...that way we could co-parent and everything wouldn't be on you," he said.
I didn't expect things to go this way; I just thought he'd visit every now and then and call often. He's really serious. I mean, he's REALLY

serious about making things right with our kids if he's willing to move across the world.

"Let God lead you and then make the decision," I said.

"For sure! Hey, my lawyer is calling me. It was great talking with you and the kids. I'll call them again tonight. I'll ask God if I should move, and I'll let you know. It feels good to move past everything and move forward, you know? But we'll talk soon, okay?"

"Okay," I said.

"Alright, bye," he said.

"Bye," I said.

Wow! I'm just amazed! I'm in awe at the turn of events! God is so good. I'm so grateful he reconciled my kids with their father. I know that a face-to-face meeting with him will give them the healing they need because they were ecstatic to talk with him on the phone. I'm just grateful we can all finally move forward.

# Chapter 12
## *Moving Forward*

I am amazed at how God turned everything around. I went from being in a broken place of feeling lost with no hope, to being in a place of complete joy and happiness. I'm happy, my kids are happy, and life's the best it's ever been because I have been changed from within by God Almighty. Not only has He changed my heart, but He's also changed those around me. I'm especially grateful for what He's done in Aaron's life. Don't get me wrong, he acts strange when he's around me at times, and he's definitely a work in progress, but aren't we all? We've never fully arrived yet, and we never will, because there's always room for growth and improvement.

I am pleased to announce that Aaron made good on his promise and visited the kids as often as he could. He even moved to California to be closer to them and to get away from all the drama and craziness that surrounded him back in New York. As far as things go with him and me, we're cordial. Everything's strictly about the well-being of our kids. As far as things go with Tyler and me, we're just friends, and I think we'll remain just friends. I mean, with Rhonda in and out of his ear telling him who knows what, I realized he was too fickle for me, and that's not someone who I needed around my kids and me. I realized it would be better for me to remain single (unless the Lord saw fit to send me a husband) so I could focus on growing my faith in the Lord, raising my young kings and queen, and being the best me I could possibly be.

Things have really turned around for my family as well. We're just all in a better place than we were at the beginning of this story. The church is growing and flourishing with people who were really after God's own heart, and I've even seen a change in my brothers! MY BROTHERS! They're definitely not as crazy as they were in the past. They still have their slip-ups every now and then, but there's definitely a difference in them, and for that I'm grateful. I'm grateful for God's tender loving-kindness and mercies that are new EVERY morning. Man, I've said it a thousand times, but I REALLY AM GRATEFUL! Can't you tell? Out of the darkness that once surrounded me came light, life, salvation, and joy! I truly believe everything happens for a reason, and now that I look back on everything, I'm grateful it all happened the way it did because it led us all to Christ. I'm beyond excited for the future God has for my family and me because I know it's bright.

We are not our pasts. Our pasts do not define us. We are who God says we are, and we are His sons and daughters who are fearfully and wonderfully made by Him. Our past is GONE, our FUTURE is WAITING, and we're MOVING FORWARD! I've truly found beauty in disaster!

# Fast Forward 20 Years:
# Present Day 2019
## *A Peek into Our Future*

Tyler bossed up; we got married and had three sons: Trey (16), Tyler Jr. (12), and Chandler (9), bringing us to a total of six kids. Aaron and Tyler didn't always see eye-to-eye when it came to the kids, so they butted heads a lot, and I mean a lot. But other than that, we're doing pretty well. My three oldest are now grown! I still can't believe my babies are grown! And oh baby, they're doing big things. They're making waves under the power and direction of the Holy Spirit! Corbin, now 28, has his own record company, a beautiful wife named Lauren, and they will be welcoming their first child very, very soon. Calvin, now 23, and Taylor, 19, have released their first album together, and they're taking the world by storm.

I honestly never thought this would be my life. I was given another chance at love, and I'm happily married. My kids are all thriving and doing well, and I'm about to be a grandma. A GRANDMA! Don't get me wrong, everything hasn't been and isn't peachy. You all know of our past, but you have no idea what it took for us to get here, where we are now, and where we're headed. Like I said, everything's not peachy. Although Aaron turned over a new leaf and changed, we discovered some dark secrets he'd been hiding from us—secrets that are enough to rip an entire family apart and betray trust. We've suffered great opposition and endured a lot of hatred from people who don't even know us but want to harm us. This time, my kids have a story to tell. Read all about it in *Finding Beauty in Disaster Part Two*.

# Epilogue
## *Beauty in Disaster Part Two*
## *The Story Continues*

May 10, 2002, one of the happiest days of my life! On this day, I married the love of my life: Tyler Washington. I know you may be confused because I told you he was fickle because of the Rhonda situation, but guess what?! HE BOSSED UP. He quit listening to other people and listened to what God was telling him. He became the leader I knew he could be all along. He pursued and loved me like Christ pursues and loves His church. He not only fell in love with me, but he fell in love with my kids. He was a great role model for my boys, and Taylor was his absolute world. Mind you, at the time, he didn't have any kids of his own, but he always treated my kids like they were his own flesh and blood.

Now, back to May 10, 2002, it was a beautiful day, warm and sunny. The church was filled with the ones we loved; well, most of them because Tyler's family opposed him being in a relationship, let alone marrying, someone who had three kids. Anyhow, back to the wedding. The church was decorated beautifully with my favorite colors: lilac, mint green, pale yellow, and coral. My parents looked at me in awe as they prepared to walk me down the aisle for the final time. I remember looking in my father's eyes and immediately noticing something wasn't right; even the way he felt when he touched me wasn't right.

"You look absolutely beautiful, baby girl. I'm so proud of how far you have come in the Lord," Daddy said.

I began to gaze into his eyes and examine him even further. "Daddy, is everything alright? Are you feeling okay?" I asked.

Mama looked shocked and stared at both of us. Daddy hesitated to answer me and said, "I'm alright, baby girl...everything will be okay. Focus on your special day."

Something about Daddy still didn't sit well with me. I could tell something was wrong, but he insisted he was fine, and I should focus on marrying my love.

The church doors swung open as it was time for me to walk down the aisle. My eyes immediately met Tyler's. He was crying when he saw me. How sweet! I looked at my children standing beside him, and all the people in the congregation. I was overwhelmed with joy, yet I did not have peace about my father.

Our wedding ceremony was beautiful; it was an absolute dream. Then I, Tyler, the kids, and our wedding party headed outside to take pictures while everyone else headed straight to the reception. I did notice Aaron didn't show up. He told me he wasn't coming, but he also told the kids he would come to see them because they were in the wedding. It didn't bother me one bit, but it bothered them because, and I quote, "Daddy said he would come!" Nonetheless, it was a spectacular day.

It came time for us to be introduced as Mr. and Mrs. Tyler Washington at the reception. When we walked in, there were lots of cheers and the expression of joy. Then it happened, we heard a loud thud and a scream of horror, and it came from the direction where my parents were.

**If you would like to know what happened next, read Beauty in Disaster Part Two, which will be available soon.**

www.ingramcontent.com/pod-product-compliance
Lightning Source LLC
Chambersburg PA
CBHW030134260626
47156CB00008B/2947